Big
&SMALL™

THE
MYSTERIOUS
WOODS

First published in Great Britain by HarperCollins Children's Books in 2010.

13 5 7 9 10 8 6 4 2

ISBN: 978-0-00-731981-7

A CIP catalogue record for this title is available from the British Library.

The HarperCollins website address is www.harpercollins.co.uk

Based on the television series Big & Small and the original script, 'The Mysterious Woods' by Glen Berger. Adapted for this publication by Davey Moore.

© Kindle Entertainment Limited 2010.

Printed and bound in China.

HarperCollins Children's Books

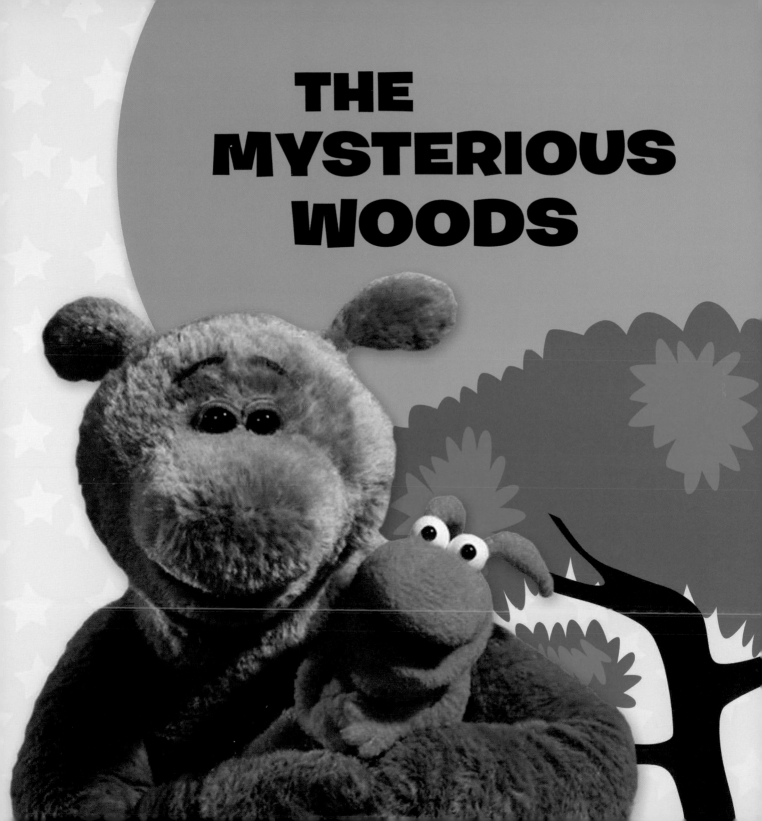

THE MYSTERIOUS WOODS

Big and Small were outside in the garden, playing with a bat and ball.

'Are you ready, Big?' asked Small.

'Yes, Small,' said Big. 'But this is the last time, because I want to go inside and finish my jigsaw.'

With all his strength, Small squashed the ball down on a big spring. When he finally let go of the ball, the spring went PING and the ball shot up into the air. Big swung his bat and hit the ball - **THWACK!**

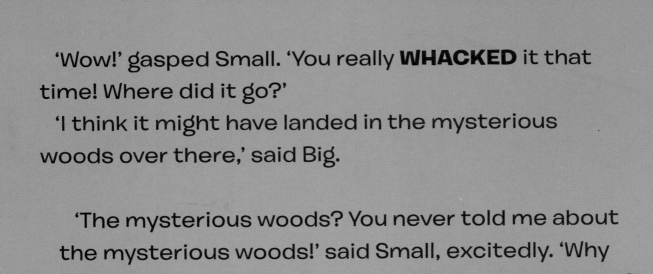

'Wow!' gasped Small. 'You really **WHACKED** it that time! Where did it go?'

'I think it might have landed in the mysterious woods over there,' said Big.

'The mysterious woods? You never told me about the mysterious woods!' said Small, excitedly. 'Why are they called the mysterious woods?'
'Because I've never been there,' said Big. And off he went to finish his jigsaw, leaving Small to wonder about...

THE MYSTEEERIIIOUS WOOOODS!

Inside the house, Big was busy with his jigsaw.

Small looked thoughtful and said, 'I was just thinking that getting our ball back from the mysterious woods could be the adventure of a lifetime!'

'We don't have to go into the mysterious woods to have an adventure!' said Big. 'We can have an adventure right here.'

'But everything's always the same in this room,' said Small. 'Don't you want to go somewhere new and different?'

We can't just shoe-horn televisions we don't like.
Big, we don't have any televisions. Small, sorry, I don't
I don't know what Big Television's about.
Televisions are the things you eat dinner down when
I don't want a television! We want television and we want
present and we want television and we want television!

Small sped off and came back
in a flash with a wagon-load of stuff.
'There you go, Big,' he said.
'Provisions!'

We've got
everything we need
for an adventure - celery,
trumpet, sandwiches,
emergency moustaches,
cow in a can...

'You forgot the most important thing,' said Big. 'A map.'

'Ta-daah!' said Small.

'One map of the mysterious woods!'
'Hey!' said Big. 'Where did you get this?'
'I made it!' said Small. 'I drew the big wheel and I drew the boat and I drew some scary alligators.'

'I'm pretty sure there's no big wheel
in the mysterious woods,' said Big.
'How do you know?' said Small.
'Come on! Let's go and find our
ball before the alligators eat it!'
'I'm pretty sure there aren't
any alligators, either!' said Big.

Big and Small reached the end of the garden. They both said at the same time...

'THE MYSTERIOUS WOODS!'

Small climbed up onto Big's shoulder so he could get a better view.

'I can't see a boat, Small,' said Big. 'I think there might be something wrong with your map!'

'There's nothing wrong with my map,' said Small, hopping down and walking off into the woods with the map. 'You just have to read it the right way! Let me show you.'

While Small walked away with the map, Big spotted something and wanderered off in the other direction.

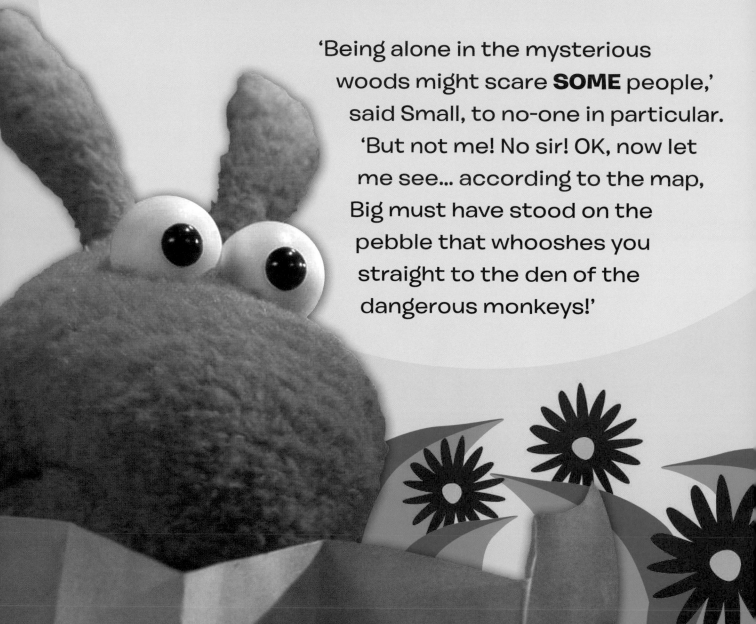

Small looked up from the map. 'I know where we are!' he said. 'I think we're somewhere near the grotto of gremlins.' And he looked around. But Big was nowhere to be found. Small was all alone.

'Being alone in the mysterious woods might scare **SOME** people,' said Small, to no-one in particular. 'But not me! No sir! OK, now let me see... according to the map, Big must have stood on the pebble that whooshes you straight to the den of the dangerous monkeys!'

'Don't panic, Big!'
said Small, grabbing a
stick of celery from the
provisions. 'I'll save you!'
And off he rushed...
a little deeper into the
mysterious woods!

'Small!'

shouted Big, coming back to the wagon of provisions. He was looking for Small but, of course, Small had just rushed away!

'I found the ball!' said Big. He put the ball into the wagon by the emergency moustaches, then wandered off to look for Small.

Small returned to the wagon, waving his stick of celery like a sword.

'Huh,' huffed Small, 'No sign of Big - and I looked under every leaf I could find!' And that's when Small spotted the ball, in among the provisions.

'That's the ball we've been looking for!' said Small. 'How did it get here?' He thought hard. 'There's only one explanation,' he said. 'Big hit the ball really, really, really high - so high that it didn't land until now - and it landed right in our wagon!'

Just then a woodpecker had a good old peck at a tree trunk –

rat-a-tat-a-tat!

And a friendly black crow had a bit of a sing-song –

squawk squawky SQUAAAWK!

Perfectly normal things in a mysterious wood – but Small didn't know that!

'**Argh!** Wild animals!' panicked Small, shaking up the cow-in-a-can. 'Get back! I have a cow!' And he ran away and hid!

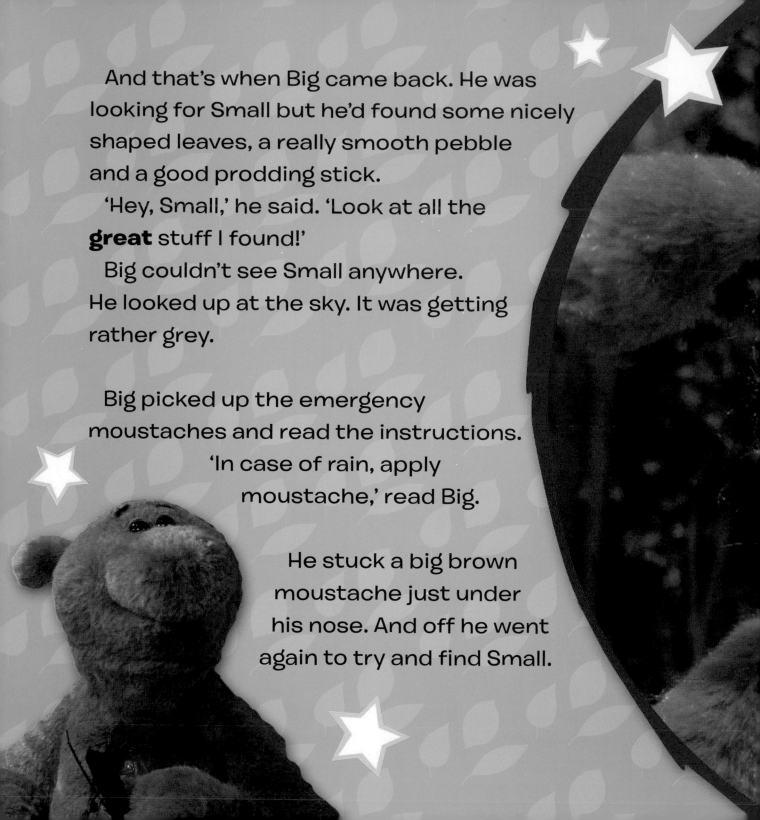

And that's when Big came back. He was looking for Small but he'd found some nicely shaped leaves, a really smooth pebble and a good prodding stick.

'Hey, Small,' he said. 'Look at all the **great** stuff I found!'

Big couldn't see Small anywhere. He looked up at the sky. It was getting rather grey.

Big picked up the emergency moustaches and read the instructions. 'In case of rain, apply moustache,' read Big.

He stuck a big brown moustache just under his nose. And off he went again to try and find Small.

And that's when Small came back! He looked up at the sky, which was crowding up with rain clouds.

'Oh no,' he said. 'Now, not only am I really scared... I mean, not only am I really **TIRED**, but now I need a moustache!'

Small rummaged around in the wagon and found a nice big, twirly moustache.

'Since I'm a bit tired, I think I'll have a little sit down,'
said Small, and he hid behind the emergency trumpet
and under an emergency box of cereal.
'Ah,' sighed Small, settling down on
top of the emergency sandwiches,
'that's better.' And it was
so comfy on those sandwiches,
that he fell asleep!

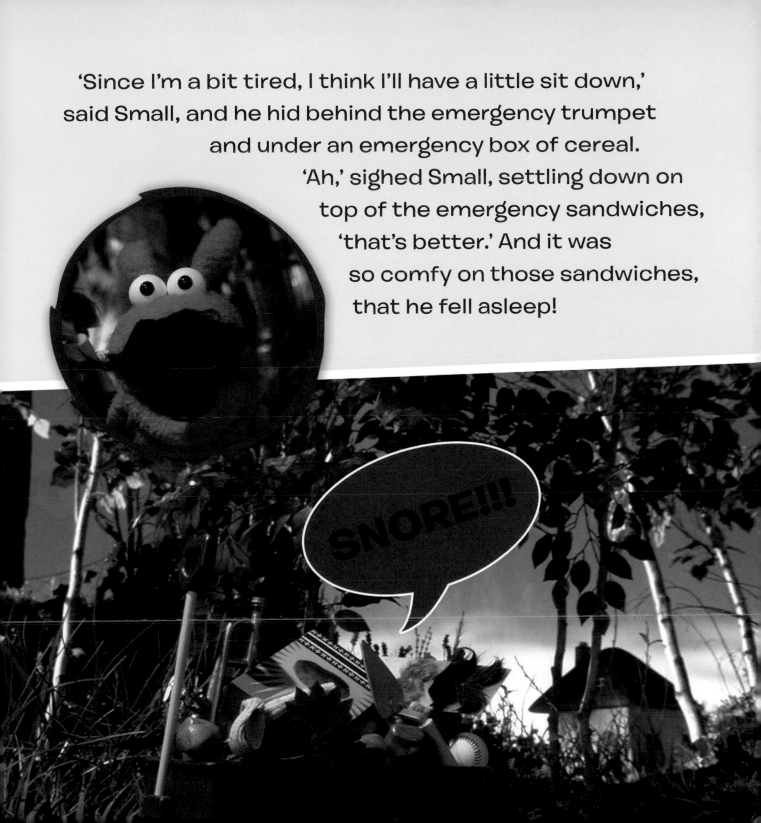

As the first few drops of rain began to fall, Big came along. He was still wearing his emergency moustache and now he was carrying his emergency lantern.

Big shouted out for Small but, when he got no reply he said, 'Oh well. I suppose I'd better get this stuff home so it doesn't get wet. I'll come back in a minute and look for Small.'

Big trundled the wagon back towards the house, holding up his lantern to light the way.

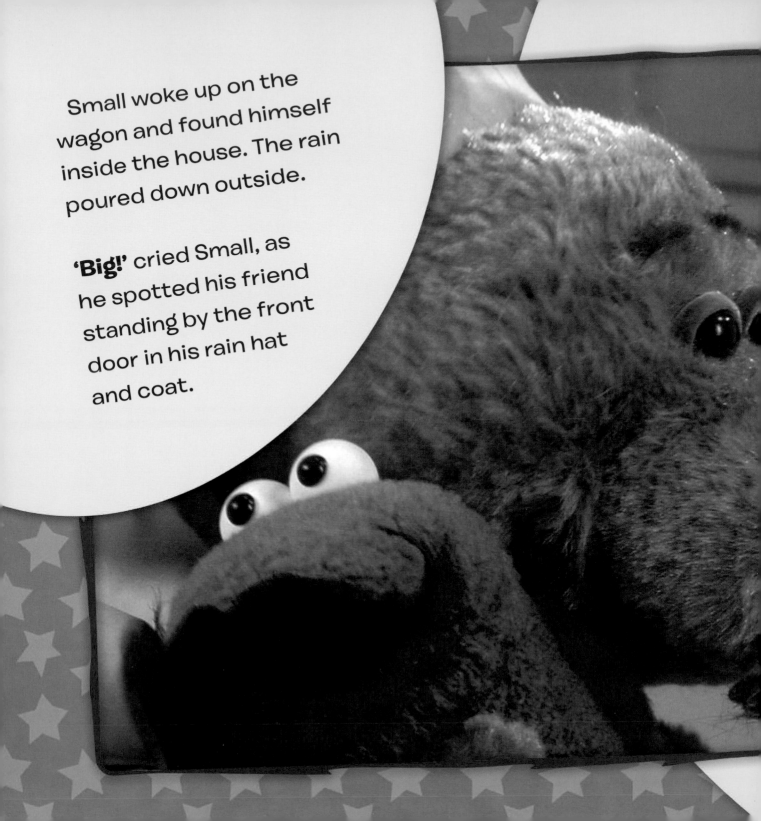

Small woke up on the wagon and found himself inside the house. The rain poured down outside.

'**Big!**' cried Small, as he spotted his friend standing by the front door in his rain hat and coat.

'**Small!**' said Big, surprised to see his pal indoors. Big and Small were so happy to see each other, they had a big hug.

'What are you doing here?' asked Big. 'I was just going outside to look for you!'

'Look for me?' said Small. 'But you're the one who got lost!'

'Me?' said Big. 'I wasn't lost, you were!'

'Oh, Big,' said Small, hugging Big back. 'I won't tell anybody how desperately lost you were before I bravely came to save you. And look!' said Small, picking something up. 'I even found our ball!'

Small twitched his moustache in triumph.

A little while later, Big and Small were wrapped up warm and dry.
They were playing a game, by the light of Big's emergency lamp.

'I was wrong about your map being no good,' said Big. 'As a board game, it takes the cake!'
'I was wrong too!' said Small. 'I didn't think we could have fun and adventure without going outside! But this is the funnest game I've ever played!'
'Nearly as much fun as emergency moustaches,' said Big, wiggling his moustache and making Small laugh.

The two friends carried on playing their Mysterious Woods board game for a long time after the rain had stopped.

Other great Big and Small books

Big & Small: THE QUITE BIG BOOK ABOUT BIG

Big & Small: THE NOT SO SMALL BOOK ABOUT SMALL

Big & Small: Smallish Library

Big & Small: MEET BIG MEET SMALL

Big & Small: QUICK, QUICK, SNOW!

Big & Small: SMALL TO THE RESCUE!

BIG & SMALL'S Busiest Day Ever
A sticky sticker storybook
With over 50 GREAT stickers!

Big & Small: SINGALONG SONG BOOK
Includes CD

Big & Small: WOWZARAMA DOODLE BOOK